EXTINCT ANIMALS

WOOLLY MAMMOTH

Aaron Carr

www.av2books.com

LET'S READ
AV²
BY WEIGL™
ADDED VALUE • AUDIO VISUAL

Go to **www.av2books.com,**
and enter this book's
unique code.

BOOK CODE

E727647

AV² by Weigl brings you media
enhanced books that support
active learning.

AV² provides enriched content that supplements and complements this book. Weigl's AV² books
strive to create inspired learning and engage young minds in a total learning experience.

Your AV² Media Enhanced books come alive with...

Audio
Listen to sections of
the book read aloud.

Video
Watch informative
video clips.

Embedded Weblinks
Gain additional information
for research.

Try This!
Complete activities and
hands-on experiments.

Key Words
Study vocabulary, and
complete a matching
word activity.

Quizzes
Test your knowledge.

Slide Show
View images and
captions, and prepare
a presentation.

... and much, much more!

Published by AV² by Weigl
350 5ᵗʰ Avenue, 59ᵗʰ Floor
New York, NY 10118

Websites: www.av2books.com   www.weigl.com

Library of Congress Control Number: 2014958682
ISBN 978-1-4896-3094-0 (hardcover)
ISBN 978-1-4896-3095-7 (softcover)
ISBN 978-1-4896-3096-4 (single-user eBook)
ISBN 978-1-4896-3097-1 (multi-user eBook)

Printed in the United States of America in Brainerd, Minnesota
1 2 3 4 5 6 7 8 9 0   19 18 17 16 15

022015
WEP021315

Project Coordinator: Aaron Carr
Art Director: Terry Paulhus

All illustrations by Jon Hughes, pixel-shack.com. Photos: page 18, Getty Images; pages 20–21, Alamy.

EXTINCT ANIMALS

WOOLLY MAMMOTH

In this book, you will learn

what its name means

where it lived

what it looked like

what it ate

and much more!

Meet the woolly mammoth.
Its name means "earth mole"
or "earth horn."

Woolly mammoths were huge animals.

They were about
the same size as elephants.

Woolly mammoths had two tusks that never stopped growing.

They used their tusks to find food buried under snow.

9

Woolly mammoths were plant eaters. A mammoth used its long nose to reach food on the ground.

Woolly mammoths moved slowly
on their four huge legs.

They had wide feet
that helped them walk on snow.

Woolly mammoths
had two layers of fur.
Short hairs kept them warm.
Long hairs kept them dry.

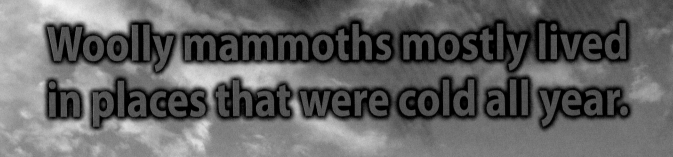

Woolly mammoths mostly lived in places that were cold all year.

They were found in Europe,
Asia, and North America.

The woolly mammoth died out more than 7,500 years ago.

People know
about mammoths
because of fossils.

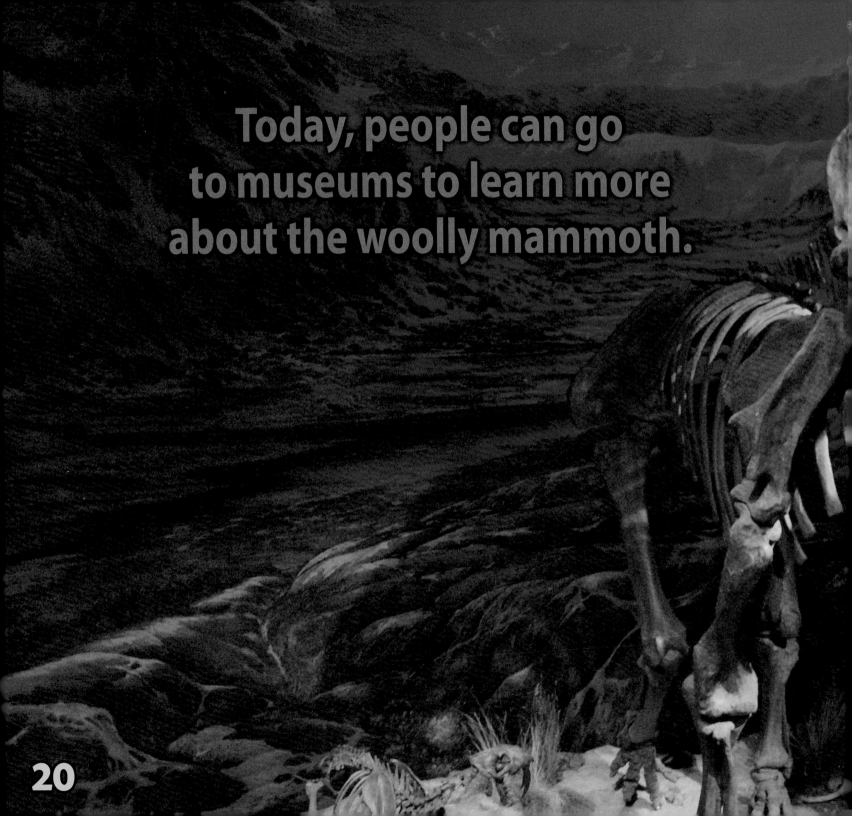

Today, people can go
to museums to learn more
about the woolly mammoth.

WOOLLY MAMMOTH FACTS

These pages provide detailed information that expands on the interesting facts found in the book. They are intended to be used by adults as a learning support to help young readers round out their knowledge of each amazing animal featured in the *Extinct Animals* series.

Pages 4–5

The name mammoth may mean "earth mole" or "earth horn." Mammoths were a genus of massive land mammals in the same family as modern-day elephants. The name "mammoth" is believed to have either come from the Estonian words *maa* and *mutt*, meaning "earth mole," or the Russian word *mamont*, which is thought to have come from a Siberian word meaning "earth horn." Since their bones were found in the ground, people believed mammoths burrowed underground like moles.

Pages 6–7

Woolly mammoths were as big as elephants. It is widely accepted that there were five species of mammoths, though some scientists have suggested there were as few as four or as many as 16. The largest mammoth species was the steppe mammoth of Eurasia, which may have reached sizes up to 15 feet (4.5 meters) tall at the shoulders. The woolly mammoth was smaller, at about 11 feet (3.5 m) tall and weighing up to 8 tons (7.3 metric tons). This is about the same size as the modern-day African elephant.

Pages 8–9

Woolly mammoths had long, curved tusks that continuously grew throughout their lives. Their tusks grew up to 9 feet (2.7 m) long, though larger species had tusks as long as 16 feet (4.9 m). Males had larger, heavier tusks than females. In addition to clearing snow to find food, it is believed mammoths use their tusks to attract mates and fend off predators, such as saber-toothed cats. Like trees, mammoth tusks have growth rings. Scientists can count these rings to determine how old a mammoth was when it died.

Pages 10–11

Woolly mammoths were herbivores, or plant-eaters. Their diet was mostly made up of various types of grass, though they ate other plants and flowers as well. Like other members of the elephant family, the woolly mammoth had a long trunk that it used to reach food in high and low places. The trunk was an elongated upper lip and nose that could be moved like an arm. It was also prehensile. This means the trunk could wrap around objects to pick them up.

Woolly mammoths moved slowly on their four huge legs.

Scientists think mammoths moved at about the same speed as modern-day elephants. This is about 15 miles (24 kilometers) per hour in short bursts or about 4 miles (6 km) an hour over longer distances. Mammoths walked on their toes. The bottom of each five-toed foot had a thick, fatty pad. These pads provided cushioning for each step. They also spread out to about 2 feet (0.6 m) wide. This helped support the mammoth's weight, allowing it to walk on snow.

Woolly mammoths had two layers of fur.
The mammoth had an inner layer of short hair that insulated the body to keep it warm. Mammoths also had an outer layer of guard hairs up to 2 feet (0.6 m) long. These hairs protected mammoths from rain and snow. Mammoths shed their inner coat during the summer and regrew it for winter. They also had a thick layer of fat and thick skin that helped to keep them warm. The fat layer was about 4 inches (10 centimeters) thick. The skin was 1 inch (2.5 cm) thick, except around the eyes and mouth.

Woolly mammoths were found in North America, Asia, and Europe.
Woolly mammoths are mostly associated with the cold tundra landscapes of the last ice age. However, they could also be found in grasslands, wetlands near rivers, and even in mountainous regions. The woolly mammoth came to North America from Europe during the last ice age. At this time, much of the Arctic was frozen, allowing woolly mammoths to walk across a temporary bridge. North America was also home to the larger Columbian mammoth.

Woolly mammoths died out about 7,500 years ago.
They lived during the later part of the Pleistocene Epoch and into the current Holocene Epoch. The first woolly mammoths roamed the area of present-day Europe about 200,000 years ago. Evidence suggests the woolly mammoth may have lived as recently as 7,600 years ago in North America. Fossils have been found in most parts of the world, and complete specimens have even been found preserved in ice.

People can go to museums to learn more about the woolly mammoth.
Each year, people visit museums around the world to see woolly mammoth fossils and life-sized recreations. Many museums, such as the American Museum of Natural History in New York City, have year-round woolly mammoth exhibits. Lyuba, the most complete mammoth ever recovered, has been touring museums around the world since it debuted at the Field Museum of Natural History in Chicago, Illinois, in 2010.

KEY WORDS

Research has shown that as much as 65 percent of all written material published in English is made up of 300 words. These 300 words cannot be taught using pictures or learned by sounding them out. They must be recognized by sight. This book contains 47 common sight words to help young readers improve their reading fluency and comprehension. This book also teaches young readers several important content words, such as proper nouns. These words are paired with pictures to aid in learning and improve understanding.

Page	Sight Words First Appearance
4	earth, its, means, name, or, the
6	animals, were
7	about, as, same, they
8	find, food, had, never, that, their, to, two, under, used
11	a, long, on, plant
12	four, moved
13	feet, them
15	of
16	all, in, lived, places, year
17	and, found
18	more, out, than
19	because, know, people
20	can, go, learn

Page	Content Words First Appearance
4	horn, mole, woolly mammoth
7	elephants
8	snow, tusks
11	eaters, ground, nose
12	legs
15	fur, hairs, layers
17	Asia, Europe, North America
19	fossils
20	museums

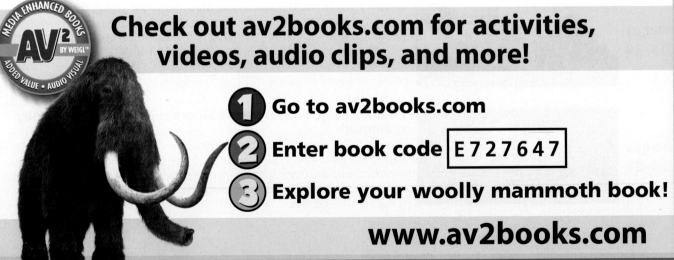
24